WINTER ICE IS NICE!

Adapted by Bob Barkly

From the television script "That's Snow Lie" by Scott Guy

Illustrated by Carolyn Bracken & Ken Edwards

Based on the Scholastic book series "Clifford The Big Red Dog" by Norman Bridwell

ISBN 0-439-38990-9

10 9 8 7 6   04 05 06

Printed in the U.S.A.
First printing, November 2002

SCHOLASTIC INC.

New York   Toronto   London   Auckland   Sydney
Mexico City   New Delhi   Hong Kong   Buenos Aires

It was winter on

Birdwell Island.

Emily Elizabeth and her

friends were playing

in the snow.

"Look out!" Charley yelled.

"Here I come!"

He went flying down the hill.

Clifford and his friends

were at the soccer field.

It was covered with ice.

"Look at me!" T-Bone said.

"I'll show you my famous

Hop, Hop, and Slide."

T-Bone ran fast.

He hopped high . . .

. . . and he slid across the ice!

"Watch me!"
Mac said.
"Hop, hop—
and slide!"

Clifford was next.

He took one hop. . . .

Oops!

He hopped too far!

Clifford began again.

But this time he went

right to the sliding part.

"Whee!" Clifford said.

"Whoa!" said T-Bone.

Clifford stopped just in time!

"That was great!" Clifford said.

"Now you go, Cleo!"

"Uh, um, okay," Cleo said.

"Here I come."

Cleo took one little step. . .

. . . and down she went.

Clifford, Mac, and T-Bone

came over.

"Are you okay?"

Clifford asked.

"Um . . . well . . . I think

I hurt my paw, " Cleo said.

"Maybe we should get Dr. Dihn,"
said T-Bone.

"No!" Cleo yelled.

"I just need to rest my paw."

Clifford made a place for Cleo

to rest.

"A snow couch!" she said. "Cool!"

Mac kept sliding. He was having fun.

Later, Clifford gave Cleo

a ride home.

"Thanks, Clifford," she said.

Cleo limped up to her house.

"Hey, Cleo," T-Bone said.

"I thought it was your

other paw that hurt."

Cleo stopped.

"Uh, um, " she said.

"Oh, no! It must be spreading!

Both my paws hurt now.

I have to go in

and lie down."

The next day Clifford,

Mac, and T-Bone went

back to Cleo's house.

Cleo was playing in the yard.

"Do you want to come skate

with us?" Clifford asked.

Cleo stopped playing.

"I don't know," she said.

"My paw still hurts."

"I thought it was your *front*

paw that hurt," Mac said.

"Huh? Oh, yeah," Cleo said.

"But don't worry.

I can still watch."

"It's funny how Cleo's
sore paw keeps moving
around," T-Bone said.
"Sure is," Mac said.

At the ice rink, Clifford

spun around and around

on his big red tail.

"Come on, guys," he said.

"This is fun."

T-Bone ran onto the ice.

But Mac stayed behind.

"I don't know how

to do that," he said.

"I'll look silly."

"Who cares?" Clifford said.

"No one does it perfect

the first time. Try it," he said.

"Okay, I'll try," Mac said.

Mac flipped and he flopped.

But soon he could spin

as fast as Clifford and T-Bone.

Cleo jumped up on all fours.

"That does look like fun,"

she said.

Suddenly, she lifted up her paw.

"Maybe your paw is better now,"

Clifford said to her.

"You know, I think you're right!"

Cleo said.

She ran to the ice.

Cleo spun around.

"Wheeee!" she cried.

"What about your sore paw?"
Mac said.

Cleo looked down.

"I didn't really hurt my

paw," she said. "I never

skated before. I was afraid

you guys would think I look silly."

"But trying new things

with your friends

is fun," Clifford said.

"And so is being silly."

"You're right!" Cleo said.

"Let's all be silly together!"

Wheeee!

Do You Remember?

Circle the right answer.

1. Clifford and his friends were playing . . .
    a. on a snowy hill.
    b. on the soccer field.
    c. at the playground.

2. What did Clifford make for Cleo?
    a. A snowman
    b. A snow couch
    c. A snowball

Which happened first?
Which happened next?
Which happened last?
Write a 1, 2, or 3 in the space after each sentence.

Cleo fell on the ice. _____

T-Bone did his famous Hop,
Hop, and Slide. _____

Clifford spun around and
around on his tail. _____

Answers:

Clifford spun around and around on his tail. (3)
T-Bone did his famous Hop, Hop, and Slide. (1)
Cleo fell on the ice. (2)
2. b
1. b